Huxton Rymer - President

by G. H. Teed

Illustrated by Eric Parker

First published in the Union Jack magazine,
Series 2, No. 1047, 3 November 1923.

Stillwoods Edition

Stillwoods.Blogspot.Ca

Catalogue Information:
Title: Huxton Rymer - President
Author: G. H. Teed (1881-1938)
Illustrated by: Eric Parker
First published anonymously in the Union Jack magazine, Series 2, No. 1047, 3 November 1923.
This Edition by: Stillwoods, 2021, (Doug Frizzle)
ISBN Canada: 978-1-989788-50-9
Blog: Stillwoods.Blogspot.Ca
Author Blog: http://ghteed.blogspot.com/
Storefront: http://www.lulu.com/spotlight/lulubook22

Keywords: Sexton Blake, British fictional detective, Tinker, Dr. Huxton Rymer, Costa Bueno (Costa Rica)

Teed Bibliography Link:
https://tinyurl.com/ve25d42s
The link above should go to a spreadsheet of all known Teed stories. The list is annotated with various information on the stories and my progress with recapturing the work.   /drf

Cautionary Note: This series of books by Stillwoods are intended to make the stories of G. H. Teed, born in New Brunswick, Canada, available to collectors and researchers. The editor, or rather digitizer has not altered the original publication.

This story may contain language and racial terms that are not appropriate to today. I apologize for them; I know that the author was using his voice to excite and entertain an adventurous English audience. These works were published from 82 to 110 years ago. Most every work has characters of redeeming ethnicity within.

I hope you enjoy and share these stories; I have.
Doug Frizzle

Recent stories published on Lulu.Com

The Lizard Man
The Mystery of the Painted Slippers
The Eight-Pointed Star
The Straits of Mystery
The Black Jewel Case
The Detective Airman
The Soap Salvors
The Voodoo Curse
At the Full of the Moon
The Case of the Six Rubber Balls
The Loyalty of Nirvana
Tinker's Secret
A Mystery of the Mountains
The Invisible Ray
The Case of the Crimson Terror
The Secret Hand
Presumed Dead
The Twilight Feather Case
Sexton Blake in Manchuria
Revolt
Lost in the Legion
Planned from Paris
Pearls of Peril
The Shuttered Room
Sinister Mill
Shanghaied
Blackmail
Forestalled
Jungle Justice
The Man from Devil's Island
Doomed to Devil's Island
The Cryptogram -W M Graydon
The Mystery of Walla Walla
Hunted Down
The Night Operator -Packard
The Blue God

A Rail Car /drf

This story will fulfil your ideas of what a really good, gripping detective story should be. We think that the standard set in the U. J. Sexton Blake stories cannot be equalled elsewhere—and we endeavour to justify that belief by printing nothing that falls shod of typical U. J. quality. This particular yarn, written by a man who has been on the spot and knows what he is talking about, is rather better than usual, if anything. We will not shout its praises; we will leave you to be the judge. If you think you can honestly recommend such yarns as this to your friends, please do so.

HUXTON RYMER— PRESIDENT

This story will fulfil your ideas of what a really good, gripping detective story should be. We think that the standard set in the U. J. Sexton Blake stories cannot be equalled elsewhere—and we endeavour to justify that belief by printing nothing that falls short of typical U. J. quality. This particular yarn, written by a man who has been on the spot and knows what he is talking about, is rather better than usual, if anything. We will not shout its praises; we will leave you to be the judge. If you think you can honestly recommend such yarns as this to your friends, please do so.

HIS EXCELLENCY GENERAL PORFIRIO GOMEZ, President of the Republic of Costa Buena and commander-in-chief of the army of the republic, was on the horns of a dilemma.

In his private bureau in the presidential mansion in San Jose, the capital, he was seated at his desk nervously gnawing the end of a pencil. In front of him were several sheets of paper, all nearly covered by pencilled calculations. But, although he had been scribbling for the best part of the evening, the president appeared unable to find a solution of the problem which confronted him.

The problem was this:

The Treasury was empty. The army had received no pay for more than three months. The various government services were in a similar plight. And anyone who has any knowledge of the various Central American republics knows what that means. Put plainly, in the case of Costa Buena it meant that unless the president "raised the wind" very soon he would fall, and, in such a contingency, he had a shrewd idea that not only would he fall but he stood an excellent chance of being backed up against a wall and filled full of lead. Needless to say, the latter possibility did not commend itself to President Gomez.

That was precisely what had happened to his predecessor, and it didn't have any soothing effect when he considered that it was he himself who had inspired that particular firing party. It is one of the simple methods they have in Costa Buena of settling claims to the presidential chair.

And the worst of it all was that President Gomez couldn't see the vestige of a chance of raising more than about one-third the amount needed to satisfy the various claims. He knew he would not find much difficulty in staving off the various civil departments by a payment on account. But the army— that was a very different matter!

In Costa Buena no president could hold power without the support of the army. No one knew that better than General Gomez, who had fomented the last revolution. While he was nominally commander-in-chief, and before his access to power had been actively so, the duties of his office had obliged him to delegate the active control of the forces to the next of rank, General Montero. And President Gomez knew perfectly well that General Montero had been engaged for some weeks in breeding unrest among the troops.

In other words, General Montero was on the point of leading a fresh revolution which would give him his turn of the presidential chair. And unless sufficient money to pay at least three-quarters of the back pay due was forthcoming within forty-eight hours, the president knew as surely as he sat at his desk that as an insurance risk he could be quoted at one hundred per cent premium.

There had been a Cabinet meeting that afternoon at which General Montero had intimated courteously but firmly that unless a substantial amount was forthcoming within a day or two he could not answer for the loyalty of the army. He had, of course, proclaimed his own devotion to the person of the president, but the president didn't need anyone to tell him just what General Montero meant.

Claims in all, including the pay due to the various civil services, totalled close on five hundred thousand colones, which, stated in pounds sterling, meant something like fifty thousand pounds. And the utmost that the president could lay his hands on was a trifle over twenty thousand pounds.

That was a fairly large amount, but President Gomez hadn't the faintest intention of dissipating so much good cash on such worthless baggage as the tattered army of the republic. General Montero hadn't the slightest notion that there was anything like that sum in the Treasury. In fact, no one in the government knew it except the president and his brother, Senor Jose Gomez, Secretary to the Treasury.

The bulk of this sum, twenty thousand pounds, to be exact, had been received only a few days previously in consideration of a banana concession which the president had given to an American commercial firm, unknown to the other members of the cabinet. He had known at the time that eventually he must disclose this fact, but he had been hoping against hope that certain taxes would come in with which he could meet the claims of the army. With the troops behind him, he had no fear of unkind criticism on the part of colleagues.

Those taxes, however, had not materialised, and he was now faced with the extremely unpleasant alternative of using the money which he and his brother had planned to divide between them. And that thought by no means appealed to the president.

Yet, no matter how many calculations he might make—no matter how desperately he might plan, the result was invariably the same. And the president was just calculating what his chances of escaping a firing party were when the door of his cabinet opened, and a short, swarthy man entered. So like was he to the president in appearance that one would have known at once that they must be brothers, which, indeed, they were, for the newcomer was Senor Jose Gomez, secretary to the alleged depleted treasury.

The president glanced up with a faint air of surprise.

"I did not expect you so soon, my brother," he said. "I had heard that the train was delayed owing to a landslide at Las Vegas."

"That is so, but I crossed the slide on foot, and requisitioned an engine and caboose. There was no time to lose."

"Ah! You have news, then?"

Before answering, Jose Gomez glanced swiftly round the room; then he got to his feet, and with panther tread crossed to the door through which he had just entered. He jerked the door open and peered out into the passage. Apparently satisfied that there was no one eavesdropping, he closed and locked the door, returned to the chair by the desk, and, after lighting a yellow-wrapped cigarette, nodded in answer to the question the president had asked.

"I have news," he said, in a low tone. "I have found the man we need, Porfirio!"

A flicker of hope came into the dark eyes of the president.

"Are you certain?" he whispered quickly.

"Perfectly! But there is no time to lose. Since I left here two days ago for Puerta Barrios I have not been idle a single moment. As you recall, it was my suggestion that I try to find some foreign adventurer at Puerta Barrios who would do what we wished. I was convinced then, and I am convinced even more so now, that flight is our only chance. There are already mutterings at Puerta Barrios which reached my ears. Montero has done his work well on the coast."

"Carramba! That is bad hearing. What shall we do?"

"Run. as I said," responded his brother coolly.

"But our families—"

"They can follow. They will not be in danger. But if we stay we shall most certainly be stood up against a wall and shot. For myself, the prospect is not pleasing. We can get away if we act at once. In three days, two days, it will be too late. The trap is all set. The day after to-morrow, when you fail to satisfy the cabinet that the money will be forthcoming, the storm will break. And we cannot carry a single regiment with us."

"That is true," admitted the president. "But you say you have found a man who will do what we wish. Can you trust him? Or will he betray us?"

"That is a risk we must take. He has agreed to get us away from Puerta Barrios for a certain sum. It is high, but we must pay it."

"How much does the robber demand?"

"Ten thousand dollars—gold."

"Carramba! We have only a hundred thousand to share between us. That will leave less than ninety thousand dollars by the time we get away."

"To get away with ninety thousand is better than being filled with lead," responded his brother dryly.

"You are right, Jose—you are right. But this fellow—where is he? How do we know he can do what he promises?"

"I am satisfied on that score. I have heard of him before. He is an adventurer, and we have far too many in Central America, but he is not the ordinary type. I know of some of the things he has done, and it is lucky for us that I was able to find a man of his type in Puerta Barrios. But as I have brought him with me, you can judge for yourself. Shall I bring him in?"

"Yes—yes, Jose; bring him in! Let us talk together, and see what can be done."

The secretary nodded and rose. He crossed the room, opened the door, and disappeared. In less than five minutes, however, he was back, accompanied by a big, bearded man, who was dressed in a rough khaki riding-suit. He towered above the two small Central Americans, and, in the solid bulk of the northerner, the anxious president seemed to find some reassurance.

He glanced up with what was intended to be a gracious smile, and as his brother presented the visitor, he said:

"Dr. 'Uxton Rymer, ees it? I am glad to welcome you as a visitor to San Jose, senor. Be seated, I entreat you, and permit me to offer you some refreshment."

And Dr. Huxton Rymer, adventurer and crook, who was figuring just how he could turn the present Government crisis of Costa Buena to his own benefit, suavely bowed and accepted the invitation.

THE president studied Rymer for a few minutes before he broached the subject which had caused him to send his brother to Puerta Barrios. Then he said:

"Will you understand sufficiently if I speak in Spanish, senor?"

Rymer inclined his head.

"Quite, your Excellency."

"My brother has told you something of—er—of why he went to Puerta Barrios?"

"A little, your Excellency. But I have yet to hear further details before I can give a final answer."

"Yes. You understand, then, something of our present difficulties?"

"Yes. I understand, your Excellency, that you and your brother wish to get away from Costa Buena unobserved by your political opponents."

"Exactly; but only for a time, just until the present trouble blows over."

Rymer, who understood a lot more of the predicament they were in than he cared to acknowledge, had his own thoughts about that latter statement, but he only nodded in apparent agreement.

"And my brother informs me, senor, that you think you could manage this for us."

"That all depends, your Excellency. May I ask where you would prefer to go?"

"Anywhere away from Costa Buenan territory now, and afterwards on to New Orleans. But if you arranged the first part, we could arrange the second ourselves."

"You would be satisfied to be landed at, say, Bluefields, on the coast of Nicaragua, or perhaps on a passing banana-steamer which could take you straight on to New Orleans?"

"Either would suit very well."

"It could be managed, your Excellency. But, of course, you understand a certain amount of money would be necessary."

"Yes. My brother has mentioned that. The amount you named would be satisfactory."

"Then I think I can suggest something. I have been thinking it over on the way up from Puerta Barrios, and I have a suggestion to make.

"In Puerta Barrios you have a small Government motor-launch, which is used for coast-inspection work."

"Yes; the Santa Rosa."

"That is the craft, your Excellency. I have noticed her running about the harbour, and I think I am correct in saying that she carries a crew of five."

"That, I believe, is the number, is it not, Jose?"

The secretary to the depleted treasury nodded.

"Can they be depended on?" continued Rymer.

The secretary answered this question. "They might, or they might not," he said. "It all depends on whether they are already disaffected."

"Then it would be best to consider that they could not be depended on," commented Rymer. "In that case, I should have to take pains to see that they did not betray us. That will not be difficult. There are in Puerta Barrios two men on whom I know I can depend —one is an American, and the other an Englishman. They are, what is generally termed, soldiers of fortune, and they would join me in this plan. With their assistance, I should experience no difficulty in handling the crew of the motor-launch.

"Now, this is my idea, your Excellency. Your brother is aware that I am a surgeon of considerable experience, and have also devoted much of my time to scientific research. I have published my conclusions from time to time under the name of Professor Andrew Butterfield, and, since but few persons in Costa Buena know me under the name of Rymer, it will be easy for me to assume the name of Professor Butterfield.

"Let us say that I have come to Costa Buena to make a collection of butterflies and moths, which would be a perfectly natural object in visiting the country, since many unknown varieties abound here, and few of them have ever been catalogued. We will say that I have come under my scientific name of Professor Andrew Butterfield, with letters of introduction to your Excellency.

"I met your brother in Puerta Barrios, and, at his invitation, accompanied him to San Jose. On my arrival here. I was received by your Excellency, and when you found out why I was visiting your country, you offered to place at my disposal the Government motor-launch at Puerta Barrios, in order that I might run down the coast in search of specimens. Could that be arranged?"

"Easily. The idea sounds good, senor."

"Very well. I shall take two companions on board —the two of whom I have spoken. I shall run down the coast, and actually begin to collect specimens. That will allay any suspicion. Then, on a given day or night, at a given spot, I can pick up your Excellency and your brother and transfer you either to a banana-boat on its way up the coast, or else run you down to Bluefields. I know of one banana-boat which is coming up from Bocas del Toro, and is due to pass Puerta Barrios in six days. I could ascertain the exact time of her passing, and if you and your brother could manage your —er —departure for that time I think we could handle things so there would be no hitch.''

"Six days —that is a little long, senor. There will be a cabinet meeting in two days. That is the difficulty."

"I take it there must be one chief instigator of your difficulties, your Excellency. With your permission, I shall speak more plainly. In Puerta Barrios I have heard rumours that a revolution is impending, and that it is being fomented by General Montero, the commander-in-chief of the army."

"Alas! It is too true, senor."

"Then the tactics of General Montero are what you have to contend with at the next cabinet meeting?"

"Yes."

"Could you handle the other members of the cabinet if the general did not appear at the meeting?"

"It should be possible —yes. Do you not think so, Jose?"

"Yes; we could manage."

"In that case, your Excellency, I think I can promise you that you will have nothing to fear from General Montero the day of the cabinet meeting. I am willing to give you an undertaking that he will not appear. Under those circumstances, you can arrange your departure as I suggest?"

"Undoubtedly."

"Then I think we should go ahead on that basis. Early to-morrow morning I shall telegraph my two men in Puerta Barrios to come on to San Jose at once. They will reach here to-morrow afternoon. In the meantime, if you will make out an official document, placing the Santa Rosa at my disposal, I can start things moving in Puerta Barrios. And —er —I regret to say that, as I am a little short of ready money at the moment, it will be necessary for me to be provided with some funds on account."

"Senor, are you sure you can do this that you promise?"

Rymer shrugged.

"If I promise you that I shall get you safely out of the country, I shall keep my word. If I tell you that General Montero will not appear at the cabinet meeting two days hence, he will not appear. Nor will any suspicion be cast upon you by his non-appearance. If you do not care to accept my word, then we need say no more, your Excellency."

"No, no, no, senor!" cried the president, "You mistake me. I do accept your word, and I trust you to do as you say. How much money would you like, senor?

"I think about ten thousand colones will be enough." replied Rymer carelessly.

The president winced at the casual way in which the adventurer spoke of such a sum, but he rose at once, saying:

"I shall bring it to you, senor."

He left the room, and during his absence Rymer questioned Jose Gomez at some length about General Montero, about his habits, his possessions, his political connections, and so on. By the time the president returned with the money he knew a good deal about the commander-in-chief of the army, and what he learned only convinced him the more that he could make good his boast that the general would not attend the cabinet meeting.

Huxton Rymer had played the game of swiftly moving Central American politics too often in the past not to feel fairly certain of his ground—with sufficient money to back him.

But had either the president or his brother seen him a little later as he left the palace they would have been somewhat puzzled, for he was chuckling to himself in evident enjoyment; and they would have been even more puzzled if they could have heard his unspoken thoughts.

"It shall be done, my dear funky president! Both you and your brother will be got safely out of the country. And, unless I miss my guess, you are going to have a companion in your travels. I'd like to know just how much boodle you are going to take with you, but that can wait—that can wait. The first thing to do is to get a bottle of wine, and figure out just what proposition to put up to those two soldiers of fortune down in Puerta Barrios. They'll jump at the chance, and, if things break right, the three of us ought to make a very nice little clean-up here."

And with that Rymer patted the packet of colones in a satisfied way, and turned into the Hotel Atlantida, where he was staying.

The Third Chapter.   The Specialist Lays His Plans.

WITH half a bottle of rare old vintage under his belt, Huxton Rymer's fertile brain began to function freely; and before he was ready to retire that night he had fixed on the preliminary steps of his scheme to get the president and his brother out of the country, and to pull off one or two other items on his own account.

His first act was to draft out a telegram to the two international adventurers who were doing the Micawber stunt down in Puerta Barrios. In short, they were waiting for something to turn up. The something was the telegram. Rymer had no doubts that the message would bring them up to San Jose on the following day's train. Then he wrote out a notice to be inserted in the morning edition of the "Correggio," the one and only daily journal published in San Jose.

This message referred to the arrival in Costa Buena of the noted scientist, Professor Andrew Butterfield, who was visiting the country in order to make a detailed study of the butterflies and moths of that portion of Central America, and who was to be received by President Gomez and other prominent Costa Buenans, to whom he carried letters of introduction.

The notice went on to speak of the past work of the learned professor, and to quote extracts from several abstruse papers which he had read before various scientific bodies. Rymer did not turn a hair while he was writing it, and, since the scientific references were literally true, there was no mistake made in the extracts given. He despatched this, together with fifty colones in money, to the office of the paper, then he set himself to a more difficult task.

This was the composition of a letter to General Montero, the commander-in-chief of the army of the republic, and one of the largest landholders in the country. Rymer spent a good deal of time over this, for he knew the most difficult part of his whole task would be to entice Montero into the trap he was setting.

His final effort was as follows:

"To His Excellency (General de Castro y Valegas y Montero, Commander-In-Chief of the Army of the Republic, Casa Montero, San Jose, C.B.

"Your Excellency,—I hasten to address myself to your Excellency in order to pay my humble respects to one whose name is revered throughout the world as one of the greatest military geniuses of the age, and also as one who has read with the most profound admiration your Excellency's wonderful and enlightening book on 'Mistakes of European Generals in the Great War.'

"I am but a humble member of the vast body of persons who feel that the last great conflict would have been very materially shortened had your Excellency been in supreme command of the armies of either side, and, although I have lost—due to theft—certain letters of introduction to high personages in Costa Buena, including one to your Excellency—which was given me by your illustrious admirer, Marshal X,—I devoutly hope you will grant me an interview, pending the arrival of a copy of the letter for which I have cabled.

"Since it is well known to me that your Excellency has spared the time, even in such a busy life, to give your patronage to various learned bodies, it is possible that my own humble accomplishments in the field of scientific research are not altogether unknown to you. In order to recall myself to your Excellency's mind, I am taking the liberty of sending with this letter a few scientific journals containing a few of my papers.

"Aside from the hope of meeting your Excellency, my purpose in visiting your great and glorious country is to make a study of the butterflies and moths of this part of Central America, and to present the results of my labours to the British Museum. I should consider it a very great honour if your Excellency would extend the patronage and lustre of your great name to be identified with the collection. It is also my purpose to write a full treatise on this class of fauna of Costa Buena, and I crave your Excellency's permission to dedicate the book to your Excellency.

"My preliminary researches have led me to believe that among your Excellency's vast estates, there is great scope for the studies I propose making, and, with your Excellency's permission, I should like to make a portion of the collection within their boundaries.

"Finally, I trust your Excellency will be gracious enough to permit me to name the most striking capture of all after your Excellency.

"I have the honour to be your Excellency's most respectful and humble servant,

"(Signed) ANDREW BUTTERFIELD.

"B.A., M.A., D.Sc., etc."

When Rymer had finished that effusion, he read it over carefully.

Then his white-teeth showed in a smile.

"I don't see how much thicker I could have laid it on," he murmured, "It's about the worst I have ever attempted, but, judging from what I have been able to learn of Montero, he will lap it up like a cat lapping cream. He might fall for all of it or part of it, but, with that business about naming a butterfly after him thrown in for good measure, I'll bet he bites one bait, anyway. One thing is sure—before I go round to see him, I'll have to read a few extracts from his book on the Great War. The conceited little greaser! He knows about as much about strategy and tactics as a camel knows of sword-swallowing! And I'll bet he never heard of Professor Andrew Butterfield in his life! He'll say he has, though, and he'll read some of the papers in the journals I will send just to keep up the bluff. I'll have this sent on early in the morning, and then there is nothing to do but wait until the trap springs. Now I'll just punish the rest of that wine and have a cigar before turning in. I have an idea this is going to be a profitable deal all round for you, Rymer, my boy!"

About ten o'clock the next morning a uniformed attendant from the president's palace arrived at the hotel with a heavily embossed envelope containing an invitation to Professor Andrew Butterfield to lunch with his Excellency, President Gomez, at the palace. Rymer conveyed his respectful compliments to his Excellency, accepting the honour, and, at half-past eleven, duly presented himself. (Lunch in Costa Buena really meant breakfast, the general hour of which is eleven.)

He was ushered into a small waiting-room by a gorgeously clad orderly, whose uniform looked as if it had been abstracted from the wardrobe of the "Chocolate Soldier" musical comedy. Another similarly clad soldier came for him a few minutes later, and he was handed over to the captain of the guard, whose efforts at glittering display would have sent a Lifeguardsman into hysterics. This mincing gentleman conducted him to the garden, where his Excellency the president was waiting, attended by his brother, the Secretary to the Treasury.

After the formal greetings were over, the captain of the guard retired, and the three seated themselves at a table beneath a large shady tree. It was a charming garden, with a cheerful fountain playing in the centre, and, as his eyes wandered about him, Huxton Rymer grew more determined than ever to push ahead with the somewhat startling plot he had formed during the past forty-eight hours.

No mention was made at the meal of the secret interview that had taken place the previous evening. There were too many servants about, and so the conversation was confined to polite questions on the part of the president and his brother, and equally polite replies on the part of their guest. It was the noted professor who broached the subject of making a tour down the coast, and, almost immediately after, his Excellency offered him the use of the government motor-launch at Puerta Barrios. The visitor was profuse in his thanks, and, to show that he was not being idly polite, the president at once sent for the captain of the guard, who was instructed to convey his Excellency's wishes to his Excellency's private secretary.

Thus it was that, before the professor left, he was given a document which placed the Santa Rosa completely at his disposal for as long as he should desire. And a promise was given that instructions to this effect should be forwarded to the governor at Puerta Barrios the same day.

Step number one had been negotiated without a hitch.

On his return to the hotel Rymer found an even more heavily-embossed envelope awaiting him. The messenger was also there, and proved to be one of General Montero's A.D.C.'s, whose uniform was just as gorgeous as that of the captain of the guard at the palace. He clicked his heels and stood languidly twirling the misplaced eyebrow, which he called a moustache, while Rymer read the letter from the general.

It was couched in the most cordial terms, and invited the distinguished professor to call upon his Excellency that afternoon at half-past four. It added that a carriage would come for the guest; and, when he had finished reading it, Rymer knew that the vain little greaser had swallowed the lot, hook, bait, and sinker.

Nor was he disappointed in the results of his visit.

General Montero received him more than graciously. He was a short, stout, dark-skinned man, who tried vainly to cultivate a military swagger. He babbled and stuttered inane rubbish as Rymer laid on still more and more flattery, and he was not only graciously pleased to sponsor the distinguished professor's work in his study of the butterflies and moths of Costa Buena, but was undoubtedly greatly flattered that a treatise on the subject should be dedicated to him.

He seemed a little puzzled that his guest had not made this

request of the president, but Rymer tactfully hinted that it was not the name of the first man in the republic he wanted, but the name of the greatest; and, since Montero was quite certain that he was the greatest, that somewhat tricky question did not arise again. But, more than all, he insisted that the professor should become a guest on his numerous estates for an indefinite length of time, where every facility would be given him in his work; and, on top of that, he stated that he himself would conduct the professor to the nearest estate, some twelve miles out of San Jose.

As that was just what Rymer wanted he lost no time in accepting, and it was arranged that they should start the following morning early, before the sun should become hot.

Huxton Rymer was well pleased with himself as he drove back to the hotel in the general's carriage, nor was his satisfaction lessened when, as he strolled into the patio, he saw, seated at a table drinking native iced beer and smoking yellow cigarettes, the two adventurers he had telegraphed early that morning.

They had caught the morning train from Puerta Barrios; and, from the keenness of the glances they shot at Rymer as he approached, it was plain that they were ripe for anything.

While the valorous general still gaped at the sight of the two tall men standing in the road ahead, the " professor's " hand came up, and a pad soaked in chloroform was clapped over his mouth. (*Chapter* 4.)

The Fourth Chapter. Huxton Rymer Speeds the Parting President.

HUXTON RYMER and his two companions, Baker and Starr, had a long confidential confab in Rymer's room that evening.

All three men knew the country well, for they had adventured in it before, and, with the aid of a local map, it was not difficult for Rymer to explain what they had to do. They parted company at midnight; and after securing horses the two men, Baker and Starr, rode off into the night. As for Rymer, he still had work to do.

He had sent out to various shops for certain items which he needed, and until far into the night he worked away, devising a long-handled net, such as might be used by a butterfly collector —though a genuine collector would have noticed that it was much stronger than need be for the purpose—and a specimen box, which he fitted with other things he had purchased. It was after three when he turned in; but at six o'clock, when General Montero's carriage called, he was up and dressed, had had coffee, and was looking as fresh as new paint.

A driver and groom were on the box, and the latter had evidently been instructed that his master's guest was a person of importance, for he was most obsequious as he sprang down and opened the door. Then they drove off to pick up the general at Casa Montero, and when the puffing general had greeted his guest he climbed in, and they went rattling off along the dusty road between rows of dew-sprinkled coffee bushes, on their way to the estate of Montero's which lay nearest San Jose.

The country around San Jose is very rugged, and once one gets out of the confines of the town, very wild. Away to the east towers the great volcano of Irazu, which has blown its top off twice within a century, and each time had completely wiped out the town which had nestled on its flank. To the west, but nearer, was equally mighty Poaz, on top of which is a vast lake of liquid mud, which boils internally from the terrific heat of the fire monster in the bowels of the mountain.

Far, far to the north-east one could just glimpse Turialba, another volcano, terrible in the past but now silent, although for miles round about the great boulders lie as mute witnesses to the monstrous catapult which belched them forth. To the north was a verdant, wide-sweeping valley, very beautiful as the green of tree and bush glistened under the morning sun; and it was the isolated road along one side of this valley that the carriage was following.

As mile after mile went by the road became more and more deserted, until they passed scarcely a single peon, and by the time they reached the outer confines of the general's coffee estate they appeared quite alone in a vast sea of lovely green. Even Rymer could not but reflect what a pity it was that such a rich country should be the continual cockpit for the petty comic-opera creatures who aspired for power.

All the way out the general and his guest had been conversing affably, and shortly after they turned into the private road leading through the estate the professor began to open his specimen-box, in order to show the contents to his host.

It was while he was so engaged that the carriage was brought to an abrupt halt, and there was a sharp squeal or fright from the valorous general as he saw two tall figures standing in the road ahead.

That is about all he did see of what followed, for at that same instant the professor flipped out the cork of a bottle of chloroform, which he had placed in his specimen-box, and allowed the contents to spill on to a soft folded cloth, which had also been stuffed in the box.

Then, while the general still gaped at the sight of the masked men, the professor's hand came up and the pad of chloroform was clapped over his mouth, while an iron grip kept him from struggling.

In another movement Rymer brought up the long-handled net, which he dropped over the head of the driver on the box. A sharp pull, and the man was jerked clean out of his seat into the road, and by that time Steve Baker was holding a heavy revolver against the side of the groom, while Starr soothed the startled horses.

It had all been very simple, after all.

The driver and the groom were soon secured and bundled into the bottom of the carriage. As for General Montero, he had soon grown limp in Rymer's arms, but to be on the safe side he, too, was bound. Baker and Starr then climbed to the box, and, after stuffing their masks in their pockets, one of them took the reins.

About a hundred yards ahead a narrow, almost concealed road turned off at the right. Baker guided the horses into it and continued on for about a quarter of a mile, when they came to a small open space. Here, beneath a tree, their two saddle-animals were tethered. Starr sprang down, and, mounting one, seized the bridle-rein of the other. He then led the way, with the carriage lumbering along behind, and the little cavalcade continued in this fashion until a good dozen miles had been covered.

They stopped beside a little stream, where one of the adventurers produced some fruit and tortillas from one of the saddle-bags. The captors refreshed themselves with food, and water from the stream, then they lit cigarettes and discussed the next step.

"If I remember rightly, and if the map is correct, this road ought to lead us pretty close to Dos Hermanos," said Rymer as he cast a wary eye on the captives. "I figure we have come a good dozen miles since we turned into this road, and it isn't likely we will meet a soul on it. We were about eight miles out of San Jose when you bailed us up, so that makes, say, twenty miles. We ought to be able to do another twenty to-day if we go easy on the horses. That will bring us close to Dos Hermanos, where I can pick up a train to-morrow morning for Puerta Barrios.

"You two will have to improvise some sort of saddle for one of these carriage animals, and take his nibs along that way. If you travel steadily you ought to make Puerta Barrios by the second night. I'll have things all ready there, but, in any case, you'd better try and make that little hut we know of about four miles down the coast.

"You and his nibs will be safe there, and I'll have plenty of food ready for you. I will get hold of a couple of men I can trust to remain on guard there until you turn up. If I am not there when you show up you will know I am somewhere off the coast in the motor-launch. Then you will have nothing else to do for the next two days but sit tight and wait for the other pair to arrive."

Starr, a grey-haired soldier of fortune who had fought in every republic in Central America during the twenty years he had spent there, nodded his agreement, while Baker, a taciturn, lanky individual, gave an almost inaudible grunt.

"What about the two peons?" asked Starr after a few moment's silence.

"You leave them to me. I will settle them all right when we get to Dos Hermanos. I have a plan which I think will work—if I grease their palms. Shall we get along now?"

The other two agreed, and the procession started once more. As Rymer had prophesied, they passed scarcely a soul all day, and the few peons they did see were ignorant folk of the wild country, who knew better than display any curiosity about the senores. Such sights in that country were not unusual, and, for all the hill folk knew, another revolution might have taken place in the capital.

They reached the outskirts of the little town of Dos Hermanos shortly after dark, where they ran the carriage into some dense scrub. That done, Starr chose the better of the two carriage animals, and out of some pads in the carriage improvised a saddle for the general, who was now quite conscious and very much afraid.

He knew well enough now that he had been duped, but he hadn't the faintest notion what fate was in store for him, and he hadn't the nerve to question the three grim-faced "gringoes."

He naturally put it down to a coup which President Gomez had pulled off, and had to console himself with the promise that if he escaped he would see that Gomez was put up against a wall and shot without any unnecessary waste of time.

When Baker and Starr, with their captive perched uncomfortably on the improvised saddle, had departed along the lonely road which wound away in the direction of Puerta Barrios, Rymer turned the other carriage animal loose, and, giving it a sharp slap with his hand, sent it scampering off, knowing that it would have no difficulty in finding food and water. Then he gave his attention to the two peons, who were lying bound on the ground, eyeing him fearfully.

"Well, amigos," he said sternly, "you have seen what happened to-day. Now tell me, are you faithful to the service of your master? Speak up!"

Both peons nodded, and one whispered a husky:

"Si, senor!"

"Then it will pay you to listen," went on Rymer. "For certain private reasons, your master wishes it to appear that he has been carried off by his enemies. You can probably guess who they are. But instead of that we are his friends, and we are going to keep him safely hidden until it is time for him to reappear in San Jose. I am going to release you, but you are not to return to San Jose until you hear that your master has returned there. You will lie low somewhere, and say not one word about what has happened—not one word. Do you understand?"

"Si, senor."

"If you do," added Rymer impressively, "you will upset your master's plans, and if you spoil his plans you know what will be your fate. You will be captured and shot. On the other hand, your master has charged me to tell you that if you obey what I say you will be well rewarded on his return. Before you go I am going to give you each a hundred colones for food until it is time for you to come to San Jose. I am going there to-morrow morning, and if I hear a single word I shall inform your master as soon as he returns."

With that, he bent down and undid their bonds. They got stiffly to their feet, and stood quite passive while Rymer took out some notes and gave them to them. Apart from what he had told them, the money alone was sufficient to impress them how important it was that they keep out of sight and say nothing until their master should give them leave, for neither of them had ever seen so such money in his whole life. As in most Central American countries, the peons are little better than slaves who are bound to their masters for life, are very ignorant, and look for nothing more than a few beans, some rice and tortillas, a small hut and a few odd pence now and then to buy a cotton cloth. The condition of the average Indian coolie is infinitely better. And knowing all that, Rymer knew he had little to fear from the two peons, who held him in even greater awe than their own master.

When they had disappeared in the darkness, Rymer lit a cigarette and started on foot for Dos Hermanos. He had been there once before, and did not relish a night in the one insect-infected building which posed as an hotel. It was only a mud adobe hut of some four rooms, mostly devoted to the sale of aguardiente, or "white eye"— a terrific native liquor, about ninety per cent pure alcohol, and a creator of havoc among the lower classes of the country.

However, there was no choice for it, unless he wished to lie out of doors— which, presented even more unpleasant features in the shape of snakes, scorpions, and tarantulas. So he pushed his broad frame through the low door of the hut, and made an imperious gesture to the native woman who was seated behind a rough sort of bar, dispensing drink to a few peons and vaqueros.

The whole place became galvanised at the sight of the bearded gringo with the forbidding eye, and in what was probably the record time of her whole life the native woman had bundled out, bag and baggage, the belongings of three vaqueros who had been occupying one of the back rooms, and turned two peons on the job to clean it out for the senor.

While he waited Rymer consumed some frijoles —black beans —and rice, and some of the aguardiente, which seared his throat like a red-hot iron. Then he sat and smoked, and listened to the boastings of the vaqueros for an hour or so, after which he gave orders that he was to be called early in the morning. He threw himself down on the canvas cot fully dressed, and, despite the fact that there was an immediate onslaught on his carcass, he managed to drift off to sleep.

He breakfasted on the eternal frijoles and rice, and paced up and down restlessly, smoking, until the down train pulled in from San Jose. He climbed aboard, and as he cast his eye down the long, American type of carriage he gave an inward sigh of relief, as he found he recognised not a single soul. He took good care to seat himself just in front of a couple of Caballeros from San Jose; but, although he listened closely to their conversation the whole way to Puerta Barrios, he heard not a single mention of General Montero. From that he inferred nothing was known yet about the general's disappearance, and he was hoping that nothing would be known for a few days, he was counting on the people at the general's house in San Jose thinking that the general had simply decided to spend a few days on his estate, which was a natural enough thing, after all.

On arriving in Puerta Barrios, Rymer made straight for his lodgings —a couple of rooms in the house of a Spanish woman. Rymer did not expect Baker and Starr to show up until the following night, but he had plenty to do before their arrival. In two sons of the Spanish woman he found the men he wanted to send down the coast to the hut which he had named as a rendezvous. With them he dispatched a supply of food and drink, and, since they knew in which direction their profit lay, there was no fear that they would betray him.

When he had that off his mind he composed a carefully worded telegram to President Gomez, informing him, in a code of which he had left the president a copy, that all would be ready as soon as he and his brother should arrive, and naming a point near the hut as a rendezvous. The same evening he visited the local offices of one of the big fruit companies, where he was able to ascertain the movements of the tramp steamer which he knew to be loading bananas at Bocas del Toro, and which should be passing Puerta Barrios in the course of something like three days from then.

That was all he could do that evening. But the following morning, clad in immaculate white, he made a call upon the Governor of Puerta Barrios, and, since that gentleman had only been in office since the last revolution some ten months before, and since Rymer had been lying very low during the two weeks he had been in the town, he had no fear that the governor would recognise him as an adventurer who had been in the country before. He presented his letter from the president, and was at once assigned an officer, who was to accompany him to the harbour front and arrange for the Santa Rosa to be placed at his disposal.

There was now nothing for him to do but wait until he felt a bite on one of the numerous lines he had out. In the afternoon he received a code telegram from the president informing him that the cabinet meeting had passed off without a hitch, and that he and his brother would arrive in Puerta Barrios the following night after dark. How they would manage to get through, Rymer couldn't guess, unless they should run through by a special engine and car, unknown to the general public. That wasn't his job. Once they arrived, his responsibility would begin.

And when he received a wireless message which stated that the banana-tramp would pass Puerta Barrios at three o'clock in the morning, some thirty-six hours hence, he at once wirelessed asking if some passengers for New Orleans could be taken on if a boat was waiting outside the port.

A reply came advising him that this could be done, and immediately Rymer booked the passages. But, in view of the fact that only the president and his brother were fleeing from the country, it was odd that Rymer booked not two passages, but three!

That evening he took a trial cruise in the Santa Rosa, during which he carefully sized up the crew. When he had finished his inspection, he had little doubt that he, with the assistance of Baker and Starr, would have little difficulty in handling the five greasers if necessary.

But he need not have worried, for in the captain of the little craft he found a man who could be bribed with ease, who would do his bidding, and who would perjure himself to perdition afterwards if questioned. And what the captain would do, the crew would do. So it was a very satisfied Rymer that took himself down the coast that evening to the little, isolated hut to await the coming of his two companions with their captive. They arrived almost to the hour named, and immediately went into hiding.

Another day to wait for the president and his brother to turn up, then to spring the trap.

And at three o'clock one chilly morning a small motor-launch put out from the coast four miles below Puerta Barrios. Bound and gagged in the cabin was General Montero, whose presence was not even suspected by the two fugitives who sat up forward with Rymer, Baker, and Starr. Close beside the president was a small black handbag, for which he seemed to have a great regard, for his hand never left it. There was something in which Huxton Rymer seemed to exhibit an equal regard, and which his hand touched constantly. That was a heavy revolver, which he had placed in the right-hand pocket of his coat.

It was just about half-past three when the lights of a steamer came into view. The motor-launch slowed up and jockeyed for position until a rope was thrown to them. Then the launch was pulled in beside the tramp, which had come almost to a stop. The late secretary to the treasury was the first to go up, and immediately afterwards the president picked up his bag and started to follow. But suddenly he found the black bag jerked violently from his hand, and a cold ring of steel jammed against the back of his neck, as a steely voice hissed:

"Up you go, but the bag stays behind! Your brother will find enough money in his pocket to pay your fares to New Orleans! The rest remains with me! Now move!"

And before he could make a single protest the president found himself hoisted up and over the side. Then from the cabin two of the crew dragged the dishevelled figure of General Montero. Despite his protests, he was unbound and hoisted up after the other two, and up Rymer went after him.

On the deck the president was screaming maledictions on everyone in sight, but Rymer got the captain of the tramp by the arm and whispered a few words in his ear. Then he stuffed a thick wad of notes into the ready palm of the skipper.

"They're all crooks," he growled, "and as they seem to want to keep in touch with each other's movements, I thought they'd better travel together. Keep 'em on the move, skipper, and if they play up, make 'em work. They've got enough money to pay their fare, and this wad is extra. But don't push them off until you hit New Orleans."

"You leave it to me, friend! They're not the first crowd I've seen trying to skip out of one of these countries."

Rymer smiled in the dark, and slid over the side. The tramp began to gather speed slowly, and the little motor-launch turned its nose back towards Puerta Barrios.

And the last thing the three Costa Buenans heard as they stood staring in stupid amazement at each other was the loud, mocking laughter of a big, bearded man who stood by the wheel of the Santa Rosa, gazing towards the dark bulk of land from which he was determined to tear out a fortune before he left it again.

Suddenly the President of the Republic of Costa Buena found the black bag jerked violently from his hand and a cold ring of steel jammed against his neck. "Up you go, but the bag stays behind!" a voice whispered. "Your brother will find enough money in his pocket to pay your fares to New Orleans. The rest remains with me. Now move!" (*Chapter* 4.)

MR. SEXTON BLAKE was striding down Piccadilly when he was arrested in his course by a voice calling his name. He paused, and turned to find a big, opulent-looking Rolls-Royce drawing in to the kerb. There was a uniformed chauffeur at the wheel, and a gentleman was leaning out of the window. It was evidently he who had called Blake's name.

Blake could not recall ever having seen the individual before, but he paused until the car came to a stop. The man who had been leaning out of the window opened the door and sprang out.

"Sorry to shout you out in the middle of the street, Mr. Blake," he said briskly. "You don't know me, but I have seen you on two or three different occasions. You were pointed out to me, and I never forget a face."

And Blake, listening to the crisp voice, and regarding the extremely well-groomed but business-like figure of the gentleman who addressed him, believed him. He smiled, and said pleasantly:

"I must confess you have the advantage of me. Perhaps I should know you, but, if we have mutual friends, they have neglected to introduce us."

The other nodded, and, as he moved a little to one side, Blake spied another and younger man in the car.

"That's just it," agreed the stranger. "But I'll rectify that now. My name is Benjafield, of the Sphinx Exploration and Development Company. I want you, if possible, to drive on to my office with me."

Blake bowed.

He knew the Sphinx Company very well indeed as one of the big development firms in Central America, and knew that they controlled all sorts of exploitations out there, from railroads to gold-mines, and from banana plantations to ocean-going ships. And he knew them from another angle, for, among his various investments, he held quite a fair quantity of their debentures.

Therefore, apart from ordinary professional interest, he was a little curious to know why Mr. Benjafield, of the Sphinx Company, seemed so keen on having a talk with him. He had been bound for the Venetia—it was just after mid-day—to discuss with Harry, the barman, just what cocktail he should imbibe, a process by no means as brief as one might suppose, seeing that Harry was the most finished "mixiologist" in Europe, and carried in his head the recipes for more than three hundred palate ticklers.

And, as Blake had had a very busy morning, he felt himself entitled to that mild indulgence.

"I know your name very well, Mr. Benjafield," he said, with a smile. "In fact, I am among the debenture-holders in the Sphinx, so I know something of the firm. If you wish to consult me about something, I think I have the time now to go on to your offices."

"Good man! Will you get in? I called at your consulting-room in Baker Street, but the young man there —smart youngster, that! —told me if I hit Piccadilly near Dover Street, and drove slowly towards the Venetia, I might have a chance of picking you up. Then said, if I didn't see you, to try the Venetia bar. Seems to have your movements placed all right —what?"

Blake was inwardly amused as he stepped into the car —amused because, while Tinker had evidently been carefully impressing the business man with his astuteness as a detective, he had in reality known just about where his master could be found at that time, since it had been less than a quarter of an hour that Blake had telephoned him from his boot-makers in Dover Street, telling him that he was going to the Venetia, and would be back at Dover Street before one o'clock. However, since that phase of it couldn't affect Mr. Benjafield, he kept silent.

Once in the car, he was introduced to the other occupant, a Mr. McGregor, who, the president of the Sphinx Company informed Blake, was their senior director in the republic of Costa Buena. Then, as the door slammed and the car drove off, the president turned to Blake, and said:

"Ever been in Costa Buena, Mr. Blake?"

"Oh, yes, indeed; several times! I had the rather interesting experience some years ago of taking part, in a revolution there. But I haven't been there for about three years now, and I don't think I met Mr. McGregor the last time I was there. At that time Mr. Keith was director."

"That's right. McGregor has been there only about eighteen months. Keith died —blackwater!"

"All, I am sorry to hear that! He was a fine man, and I was grateful to him for many courtesies."

"It was Keith who first pointed you out to me in a London theatre. But to get to business, Mr. Blake, I am glad that you are a debenture-holder in the Sphinx, and also that you know Costa Buena. It will facilitate matters greatly. Can you arrange to go out there at once?"

Blake laughed.

"That is a little sudden, Mr. Benjafield," he said. "I think it would be better if I know a little more about the affair that seems to be exercising you."

"Exercising is right. You can call it financial, business, or political, or all three rolled into one if you wish. But there is trouble popping out there, and Sir Henry Fairbairn, the vice-president of the Sphinx, says you are the one man to handle it."

"That is kind of Sir Henry!" murmured Blake. "Still—"

"Yes; I know what you are going to say. You want all the particulars, and I will give them to you. Ah, here we are at the offices now! Come up, Mr. Blake. Come along McGregor! You are the one to tell Mr. Blake all about it."

Blake found that they had arrived in front of a big block of buildings in Victoria Street—an unusual location for a big general development company like the Sphinx, but very commodious and comfortable. The president's private office was on the ground floor, so they walked along the corridor and entered. As soon as they were seated in the sumptuously furnished room the president turned to the Costa Buenan director, and said, as he opened a box of cigars:

"Now then, McGregor, tell Mr. Blake the whole thing just as you told it to me. I have the docket of papers here, so if he wants to ask any questions he can consult it at once."

Mr. McGregor blew a smoke-ring into the air, then, settling himself, he said:

"It's about the present Costa Buenan government, Mr. Blake. There is the very deuce to pay out there, and while I am reluctant to make the statement, it is a fact that, unless we manage to do something soon to euchre them, our various investments in Costa Buena will be severely injured; in fact, materially reduced in value."

"The governments of those comic opera countries are always up to some mischief," remarked Blake. "I have not kept in close touch with recent political changes in Costa Buena. If I remember rightly, by last accounts, the so-called Conservatives had ousted the so-called Liberals, and one Gomez was in the presidential chair."

"Ancient history now. Neither the Liberals nor the Conservatives are in power. No regular party is in power. The country is being run by a small clique, controlled by three foreign soldiers of fortune, the leader of the trio occupying the presidential chair. And that is just where the mischief comes."

"That is a new development, even for Central America," remarked Blake. "I believe, though, it was done once in South America —in Chile —before that State was stabilised. I know a few of the soldiers of fortune who knock about those parts. What is the name of the one who has seized the reins of power?"

"His name is Butterfield, and when he first came to Costa Buena he was supposed to be a scientist, who wanted to study the fauna of the country."

"His first name doesn't happen to be Andrew, does it —Professor Andrew Butterfield?"

"It is—just that."

Sexton Blake sat up with a jerk. "Please go on, Mr. McGregor," he said. "You interest me exceedingly!"

"IF it weren't so serious for the Sphinx Company, it would be more or less of a comedy," continued McGregor. "The Gomez administration —if one could dignify it by that name —was rotten to the core, and it was about time it fell. We didn't care two straws one way or the other, for the simple reason that one crowd is as bad as the other, and any new Government couldn't have been worse than the old one —that is, any of the gangs that play at comic-opera politics in Costa Buena.

"But this trio of adventurers that is running the country is a very different cup of tea, and, unless something is done soon, things will be so chaotic that it will take years to straighten them out, not to mention the thousands of pounds it is costing us. I will explain briefly.

"The Gomez Government was about to fall. One General Montero, who was at the head of the army, was fomenting a new revolution, and the chances were he would have succeeded in his efforts, as he had the army behind him. It seems that Gomez had spent all the money in the treasury, the army hadn't been paid for months, nor had the civil services. But Gomez collected something like a hundred thousand dollars for a concession which he gave to an American group. That hit us hard, because it had been promised to us.

"Well, it seems that Gomez knew what was afoot, and decided to clear out of the country, taking with him all the money he could lay his hands on. His brother was to go with him. No one knows exactly what happened, but it appears that he fixed up something with this man, Butterfield, and his two companions, who agreed to smuggle him out. They did that all right, but they went even further. They kidnapped General Montero as well, and shipped the whole three of them to New Orleans."

Blake smiled.

"It must have been a pleasant little party," he remarked.

"By all accounts it was," agreed McGregor; "In addition to that exploit, it seems, that Butterfield took Gomez' money away from him at the last moment, and he and his two companions returned at once to San Jose, the capital.

"They went boldly to the palace, and Butterfield summoned several army officers to meet him. He showed them plenty of money, and said he proposed paying the greater portion of back pay at once to the army, on the condition that they stood behind him.

"They fell for this, and inside an hour he was made a naturalised citizen of Costa Buena, after which he was proclaimed president. His two companions were also naturalised, one being made the Secretary to the Treasury, while the other was made Minister of the Interior. That, of course, placed the whole cabinet in his hands.

"He kept his word, and paid a large sum to the troops. He promised the civil services money at an early date, and he kept his word there, too. There were lots of taxes due, which Gomez had failed to collect. Butterfield sent the troops out and collected them by force. Then he proclaimed Gomez, his brother, and Montero outlaws, and, although they have for months been making frantic efforts to communicate with friends in Costa Buena, this man, Butterfield, has had every letter confiscated and every telegram destroyed. As he controls the posts and telegraphs, that was not difficult.

"He shipped Gomez' family and Montero's family to New Orleans, and confiscated their estates. No one cared much about that, even though he was making money for himself. Nor did anyone think much when he gave concessions to American and British companies. Every Government does that. But we began to see that things were reaching a serious pass when he began to interfere with old concessions. These have always been regarded by each new Government as not to be interfered with —a sort of unwritten law among them all.

"As you know, Mr. Blake, we control the railway-lines in Costa Buena. Owing to the rapid deterioration of wood in that climate, we have to import hundreds of thousands of railway sleepers every year. These have always been admitted free of duty, but now, since this man, Butterfield, has got hold of the reins of power, he has put an import duty of two colones on each sleeper. That, as a brief calculation will show you, runs to a very large sum of money each year.

"Not satisfied with that, he has created all sorts of petty taxes, which seem insignificant in themselves, but which total a great deal. We might even have stood that, but the last straw came about two months ago when he put an export duty of three cents, gold, on every bunch of bananas shipped out.

"Now, we also control all the bananas there, and as we ship more than a million bunches every month from Puerta Barrios, this new duty amounts to more than six thousand pounds sterling each month.

We can't stand it!

"We are, of course, paying it. There is nothing else to do. But if it continues, it means that we shall have to curtail our production in Costa Buena. That would mean, of course, enormous losses to our shareholders, because it would follow, ipso facto, that we should have to run the railways at a loss. The banana traffic is the chief traffic.

"I have gone into these matters very carefully, and I am convinced that the bulk of the money collected in various ways is going into the pockets of these three adventurers. They keep doling out sufficient to the army and the civil services to keep them quiet, but they must be piling up large private fortunes, chiefly at the expense of the Sphinx Company. That was why I came to England — to place the facts before the board of directors here. And Sir Henry Fairbairn suggested that we consult you. He said that you had once successfully handled a somewhat similar case in the Republic of Colombia."

"Just what is it you want me to do?" asked Blake.

"Will you go out to Costa Buena?" Benjafield broke in.

"That would not be easy to arrange, if you mean at an early date."

"I am afraid I do —to-morrow, to be exact. One of our boats is sailing from Bristol to-morrow. Mr. McGregor is going back in her. She is scheduled to call at Madeira on the way, but if you will go we shall cancel that and have her reach Puerta Barrios at the earliest possible date."

"But I hardly see what I can do. I don't mind telling you that I have an idea I know this gentleman who calls himself Butterfield. If he is the man I think, then I am not surprised that he is making financial hay while the sun shines. I know him as one of the cleverest criminal adventurers I have ever met. But it is obvious that the only way to cure the tumour, so to say, is to remove the growth. If he controls the army, it is not going to be easy to remove him."

"That is true," said McGregor. "But if he isn't removed, then the Sphinx Company will sustain very heavy losses through no fault of its own. You, as a debenture holder, will be affected by that, Mr. Blake."

Blake nodded.

"If he controls the army, he can't very well be removed by force. The only other way would be by strategy."

"Which wouldn't be easy, as he is guarded night and day by a picked guard."

31

"Well, that might be got round," drawled Blake. "But as Gomez and Montero are exiled, and seem to be bad lots both of them, who is there you could put in the chair? Haven't they got one decent, straight man in Costa Buena whom the people would stand behind?"

"There is one—if he could be persuaded to return to politics. I refer to old General Morales—a fine, honest old fellow, who was president some years ago. But he has retired in disgust."

"Oh, yes; I remember him! He would be just the man. Well, gentlemen, I'll tell you what I will do. I'll think this matter over during the afternoon, and let you know my decision before five o'clock. If I can arrange to go out to Costa Buena I shall do so, though I doubt if I should be able to leave before the day after to-morrow."

"We can arrange to hold the steamer back," put in Benjafield quickly.

"Very well, I'll telephone you." And with that Blake took his departure.

IT was not altogether because he had a personal interest in the affairs of the Sphinx Company that Sexton Blake decided to go out to Costa Buena. To begin with, things were not very pressing in London at the time, owing to the fact that there had been one of those inexplicable lulls in crime.

Then he guessed that the man who called himself Butterfield, and had seized the reins of power in Costa Buena, was none other than Dr. Huxton Rymer. And, while Blake could not help but admire the cool audacity of the coup, he was not averse to winding up Rymer's little game, since in doing so he would terminate conditions which the Sphinx Company was finding intolerable, and by which he himself was losing money.

Then, too, he had been overworking for several months past, and he opined that the sea voyage would do him good. Needless to say, Tinker didn't hesitate a moment. When Blake put it up to him, he came back at once with:

"Sure, guv'nor! Let's go!"

So when the Sphinx boat, Amiraldo, sailed from Bristol some thirty-six hours later, Blake and Tinker were on board.

But before sailing Blake had taken the precaution to arrange with McGregor that he should adopt an alias, so he was down on the passenger-list as James Evans, and was ostensibly going out to Costa Buena in order to make an inspection of the railway-lines on behalf of the London directors.

Tinker was down on the list as Peter Strange, and was to all intents and purposes a draughtsman apprentice in the office of the expert engineer, James Evans.

The Amiraldo was not a large boat — a little over five thousand tons —and as she had been built chiefly to carry bananas between Puerta Barrios and Bristol, she had not much passenger accommodation. In fact, she could handle about a dozen passengers comfortably, and on this trip there were only eight on board. Three of these were Blake, McGregor, and Tinker. Then there was a young Englishman, who was employed in the fruit division of the Sphinx Company, who had been home on leave and was returning with his bride. There was a Spaniard, who had originally been an independent banana-planter, but who had sold his estates to the Sphinx Company and had retired to San Jose. He had with him his wife, and a daughter about seventeen years of age, a very pretty, dark-eyed Spanish girl, to whose charms Tinker succumbed —for the duration of the voyage — without a struggle.

That made up the company, and since McGregor was the senior director of the company in Costa Buena, and as it soon became obvious that the expert "engineer" and his assistant were on most friendly terms with him, they were treated with every deference, and the stewards lost no opportunity to see that they lacked for nothing.

While the Amiraldo was almost purely a cargo-boat, she had been built, as has been said, for the banana-carrying trade, and her refrigeration was of the most modern. She had been built for speed, too, and, as they were to cut out the call at Madeira, she made the run out to Puerta Barrios in the record time of fifteen days. They had perfect weather all the way, and, each in his own way, Blake and Tinker enjoyed it immensely.

On landing at Puerta Barrios, McGregor offered to place a bungalow at Blake's disposal, but this Blake vetoed. He preferred to take a couple of rooms in the official engineers' quarters, in what were once the military barracks, and situated on the seaward side of the little park opposite the Lodge —a steel-and-cement building which housed the administrative offices of the Sphinx Company on the ground floor, and the European officers on the floor above. Blake elected, too, to take his meals in the engineers' mess, in order to make his visit appear perfectly natural in every way; and, since it would not do to arouse suspicion, he arranged to see as little of McGregor as possible.

He and Tinker were soon settled in their quarters, and, since the inspection engineers in residence consisted of only a few, who were constantly changing owing to their duties keeping them out on the line most of the time, it was not difficult for Blake to sustain his role when conversing with them, since he had a considerable knowledge of railway engineering for a layman.

From the moment he had left England, Blake had allowed his beard and moustache to grow, and since that was an entirely natural proceeding on the part of one going to Central America, no one on board thought anything of it. He had also adopted regulation khaki clothes and a soft Stetson hat, so by the time he reached Costa Buena, what with these items of clothing and a promising crop of hair on his face, he looked vastly different from the spruce criminologist of

Baker Street. Tinker also wore khaki clothes, but instead of a soft hat he had chosen a white topee. As the faint down on his upper lip would not respond to coaxing, he had to pass up any idea of emulating Blake.

For the first three days after their arrival they remained in Puerta Barrios. Blake was busy getting a line on the administrative work of the railways, and what information he could on the general political situation in this country. He discovered that things were just as McGregor had said; and as far as he could make out, Huxton Rymer had fallen on about the most profitable graft of the whole of his adventurous career.

He seemed to be raking in the shekels from every possible source, and it was a certainty that a large percentage was going into the pockets of himself and his two companions.

On the other hand, he was undoubtedly running the country in an efficient manner and with an iron hand. There had been a couple of spasmodic outbreaks in San Jose which he had put down sharply, and, as he had ordered about a score of the malcontents to be shot against a wall, he had kept the situation well in hand since.

But the burden he had placed on the Sphinx Company was draining it severely, and in answer to McGregor's protests, the reply was that if any more were submitted the export duty would be raised to five cents gold on every bunch of bananas leaving the country. If the company was to be saved enormous losses, and its innocent shareholders protected —a large number consisted of widows who had invested their all in the Sphinx, owing to its high standing —the tax would have to be removed, and the only way to do that was to remove Huxton Rymer as well. That was a certainty, and at the end of three days Sexton Blake decided it would have to be done.

On the fourth day Blake and Tinker left Puerta Barrios. McGregor had supplied them with a private motor vehicle which was fitted up after the fashion of a small caravan, and equipped with flanged wheels to run on the railway metals. It could sleep three in the body if necessary, and, in addition to being fully equipped with bedding and crockery, etc., had a small oil-stove on which they could cook. In the back was a seat for a Jamaica negro "boy," who would look after them; and, since they ran on the railway on regular schedule, just like a train, it was a novel and interesting experience to Tinker. This type of motor-vehicle is used quite extensively by the inspection engineers on the railways in Central America.

Blake's idea was to take about a couple of days to make the run up from Puerta Barrios to San Jose. Along the way he would carry on his role of engineer out from England, on behalf of the English directors, and, incidentally, pick up any further information he could. In San Jose he intended to size up the situation in the camp of the enemy, so to say, after which he would communicate the result of his investigation to McGregor and submit some definite plan of action.

The first part of the run, as in several other Central American countries, was through the low banana-country which stretched in from the coast, a matter of sixty miles or so. They contented themselves with covering this much the first day, and that evening the motor-vehicle was shunted into a small siding for the night.

The stop was at a junction where the railway-line branched off, the main line continuing on up the stiff climb to the crest of the volcanic range and thence down into San Jose, while the branch, which was originally intended to be the main line, went off in a rambling direction to the north.

At the station before they got to Siquirres Junction, where they would spend the night, they had been held up for some time.

They remained there while three loaded banana-trains passed on their way to Puerta Barrios, and during the wait Blake received the extremely interesting information that a special train was coming down the branch line, carrying no less a person than the new President of the Republic, together with the Minister of the Interior and the Secretary to the Treasury.

This news made him anxious to push on to Siquirres, in the hope of seeing the presidential train pass. He had little doubts on the matter, but he wanted to get a look at the president as soon as possible, just to assure himself that in really was Rymer. Once he was certain of that, he would know better how to act.

As soon as they had been shunted into the side track, Blake and Tinker went across to the station to get news of the presidential special. By the air of excitement prevailing at the station, they knew it had not yet passed, and as soon as the station agent discovered who Blake was he at once gave him all the facilities in his power.

Just to keep the bluff going, Blake set to work, checking over some of the engineering accounts. The special was due to pass in about half an hour, so Tinker was stationed on the platform to keep an eye out for it.

When it was finally signalled, Blake took up a position where he could see without being seen, although he had little fear that a passing glimpse of his bearded features would enable Rymer —if it was he — to recognise him.

Tinker was at one end of the platform, standing behind some rough cases, when the special finally whistled for the junction. As the line had been kept clear and the points had been fixed so the special could run right into the main line and continue on its way without stopping, Tinker knew his only chance to see Rymer would be if the latter were at one of the windows, or happened to be sitting on the little observation platform at the rear of the train.

It never occurred to either him or Blake that the special might make a stop at Siquirres.

But that is just what it did do, in order to take in water. The tank was not far from the end of the platform where Tinker stood, and, as luck would have it, the end of the rear carriage, which was the one containing the presidential party, came to a stop exactly across from where Tinker was standing.

On the train were four men, three of them Europeans and one a Spaniard. In the centre of the group was a big, bearded individual whom Tinker recognised at once as Dr. Huxton Rymer.

That one glance Tinker took, then he turned to get away before he was noticed. But as he moved off the big man turned his head, and for the veriest fraction of a second their eyes met.

And, to save his life, Tinker could not have told whether Rymer had recognised him or not. But if he had been able to continue his surveillance of the train he would have seen, just before it pulled out, a swarthy man spring down from the front carriage and come sauntering back towards the junction.

Rymer had recognised him, and he had lost no time in taking steps to discover what Tinker was doing in Costa Buena, for he knew that if Tinker was there it was a pretty good bet that Sexton Blake was not far away.

As the Spaniard heard Tinker's voice he threw himself to one side like a flash, and then came up with a knife gleaming in one hand. That one glimpse Tinker had before the man's torch went out—and the next moment the intruder lunged forward. *(Chapter 8.)*

DUSK fell in all its tropical suddenness almost immediately after the presidential special left Siquirres. Tinker, who had gone round to the rear of the station, came back by making a detour, and, just as he stepped on to the platform, he noticed a short, swarthy person in earnest conversation with stationmaster, himself a mestizo.

Tinker thought nothing of it at the time, for the natives always seemed to have some pressing private affairs to discuss with each other. Nor did he see the glances which followed him as he entered the building in search of Blake.

He found Blake had returned to his work on the engineering accounts, and as he paused beside him Tinker said in a low tone:

"It was Rymer all right, guv'nor?"

Blake nodded.

"I saw him," he answered briefly. "Better go along and keep an eye on the car, my lad," he added. "It's dark, and I don't want any of these natives poking about it."

"All right, guv'nor. Will you be along soon?"

"In about a quarter of an hour. I'll finish this book for the sake of appearances."

Tinker turned and passed out again to the platform. As he reached it he saw the stationmaster checking up some goods with the aid of a couple of mestizos, but of the swarthy individual who had been talking to him there was no sign. Tinker jumped off the platform to walk the hundred yards or so to the side track where the car had been left, but scarcely had he started when he almost bumped into the Jamaica "boy" who was their servant.

"Where you off to?" he asked sharply. "I thought I told you to stay and look after things."

"Please, massa, I go 'long commissary for buy coffee. Massas maybe wanting coffee after dinner to-night."

"All right. But mind you hurry back. You should have waited until we returned."

"I come back very soon, massa."

With that the darkie disappeared, and Tinker continued his way. The black had been ready enough with an explanation, and Tinker could not know that in the pocket of his cotton bags was a bright shiny gold piece which had been given him to clear off from the car. A ten-colone piece was a lot of money to that darkie, and he was ready to lie like sin in order to earn it.

Tinker quickened his steps a little on discovering that the car had been left unguarded, although he did not for a moment think that anyone would dare to disturb their belongings. He found the side track without difficulty, and as he spotted the dark bulk of the car just ahead, he muttered an angry grunt on finding that the "boy" had gone off without lighting a single light.

At the time Tinker was wearing a pair of rope-soled "sneakers," which he had found much cooler on his feet than ordinary leather-soled shoes in the heat of the day, and, consequently, as he stepped along the hard, beaten path beside the track he made scarcely a sound.

He reached the front of the car, and then suddenly he saw the glint of a light through the front curtains which shut off the driving-seat from the main body of the vehicle.

He frowned in a puzzled way, then he went on with a stealthy tread until he had passed along to the rear of the car. As he reached it he stopped again, and twisted his head round until he could see inside; and at what his gaze encountered he gave an angry exclamation, for, kneeling inside, and working over one of their private suit-cases, was the same swarthy individual whom he had seen talking with the station-master.

"What the devil do you think you're up to?" snarled Tinker, as he landed inside the car.

His hand shot out to grasp the intruder by the scruff of the neck, for Tinker was a husky lad, and held the natives of the country in complete contempt. But his capture was not to be effected as easily as he supposed, for, as the Spaniard heard his voice, he threw himself to one side like a flash, and then came up with a knife gleaming in his hand. That one glimpse Tinker had before the torch the other had been using went out, and the next moment the Spaniard lunged forward.

Not yet did Tinker dream that the man might have come from the presidential special. Even though he had seen the knife, he could scarcely believe that the native would dare to try and use it to any real purpose.

It was a serious thing for a native to attack a white man, and Tinker at first took the knife as sheer bluff.

If he had known that the other would have had the president's protection for whatever he did, he would have realised just how serious was the situation in which he found himself. And, as a matter of fact, as the knife went slithering between his left arm and his side, ripping his shirt as it passed, he knew this was no bluff that he was up against, but the real thing.

He had no weapon on him. It had seemed entirely unnecessary to stick one in his pocket at the little junction, although, before leaving the car, Blake had dropped a small automatic in his pocket, and had said something to Tinker about doing the same. But the lad had disregarded his words, and now, as he felt that knife graze his ribs, he would have given a good deal to be able to plant a bullet in the carcass of the native.

Instead, he grappled.

He knew in an actual physical encounter he could easily handle the native, but that in the pitch dark of the interior of the car, and in such cramped quarters, a crazy native with a knife was a dangerous proposition; and Tinker knew, if he was going to prevent the other from driving that point between his ribs, he would have to use summary measures.

Tinker jammed his arm in against his side, imprisoning the other's forearm. Then he brought his right fist back, and with a stiff jab, drove it hard to the body. He felt the Spaniard give, and a grunt of pain came from him. But the effort had caused Tinker to slacken the pressure on his left arm, and as the native gave a swift pull, Tinker threw his left arm clear of the body, for he knew the old trick of turning the knife and a wicked twist on the withdrawal.

They fell apart, but before the other could gather himself together to renew the attack, Tinker took a chance on encountering the point of the knife, and, jumping in to close quarters, began driving in right, left, right, left, in a wicked tattoo that sent the native crashing against the side of the vehicle.

Then he slumped down, and Tinker sprang back as his fists encountered nothing but the hard, wooden side of the car. But if he thought he had put his man hors de combat he was mistaken, for the next instant he felt the whole leg of his trousers slit as the Spaniard gave a vicious upward slash.

Tinker went berserk.

Disregarding the knife entirely, he fell upon the Spaniard, and, getting a half-nelson on his neck, began to drive in slow, steady, sledgehammer blows that would have crumpled up a far more powerful physical specimen than that greasy Spaniard. There was only one result —there could be only one result.

The native collapsed like a pricked balloon, and began to yelp with pain.

But Tinker did not desist. As he heard the knife clatter to the floor, he dragged the man out and to his feet. Then, as he held him with his left hand, he sent his right in to the solar plexus with the whole of his weight behind it. The Spaniard dropped as if he had been shot, and Tinker staggered back panting.

"I guess that will fix the greaser," he muttered. "Now for that torch of his, and I'll truss him up until I can find out just what he was up to."

He managed to locate the torch, and when he had pressed the switch he turned the light full on to the unconscious native. He recognised him definitely now as the man he had seen talking to the station master, but he was utterly at sea to understand what the fellow had been doing in their car.

"Darned funny!" he mused. "If he is a friend of the stationmaster, then I can't understand why he was poking about in here. The stationmaster must have said something about an engineer inspector being here, and he would know what a risk he ran in interfering with our stuff,

"Queer, too, how Snowball happened to go to buy coffee just at this time. I'll have to beat that nigger up, I guess, and make him come clean with the truth. This guy is too well dressed to be a sneak-thief. Something behind it all that I don't quite grasp. Anyway, I'll truss him up, and see what the guv'nor has to say about it."

Tinker lit the small oil lamp inside the car, and dragged out some lengths of cord, which had been about part of the luggage. He made a quick job of securing the Spaniard, for the latter was beginning to show signs of returning consciousness. When he had finished, he squatted on his heels and surveyed his man closely. The lad was still deeply puzzled as to what could have been the other's object in trying to pry into their belongings. Then, as his mind went back and he remembered that brief instant during which his eyes and Rymer's had met, he muttered:

"By ginger! I wonder if Rymer did spot me? And if he did, is this the result of it? It certainly looks mighty funny to me. I wish the guv'nor would show up. He ought to know about this at once."

And just then Sexton Blake thrust his head inside the car, and gazed in startled amazement at the scene before him.

Blake climbed inside, and, lighting a cigarette, listened to what Tinker had to say. Just as the lad finished, Snowball, the Jamaica "boy," returned, and as he saw his two masters sitting over a bound captive, his eyes rolled in fear, showing the whites.

Blake made a gesture in the direction of the black.

"Beating up a nigger doesn't appeal to me, Tinker," he said curtly; "but this is a case where I think it is justified, if we can't get the truth any other way. See what he has to say."

Tinker jumped out and grasped the black by the shoulder. He gave him three chances to speak the truth, but the "boy," though terrified, persisted in denying that he had ever seen the Spaniard before. Then Tinker went to work, and gave the black a complete, though not brutal, thrashing. By the time he had finished, the "boy" was ready to tell the truth, and confessed how the Spaniard had turned up, and had given him ten colones to go off for a time and leave him there in the car.

With that to go on, Blake was able to link up several items when he had considered Tinker's story, and when he finally climbed out of the car he had made a pretty shrewd guess at the truth.

"This alters the whole proposition, Tinker," he said. "It will be no use our going to San Jose now. We will certainly prevent this greaser from reaching there to report to Rymer. But Rymer will suspect something of the truth, and our only chance is to figure up some scheme that he will fall for. The best thing for us to do is to get back to Puerta Barrios at once.

"We will take your prisoner with us, and I fancy I can arrange for McGregor to ship him down the coast and keep him out of the way for a week or so. As for the stationmaster here, I will have a talk with him now. I think I can bring some persuasion to bear to make him confess just what this fellow said to him. You keep an eye on things here, my lad. I'll go and talk with him now, and I'll arrange for a clear line into Puerta Barrios. Snowball can get dinner ready, if he can be made to stop sniffling. We shall try and get away inside an hour."

With that Blake went off, and by the time he returned dinner was ready. A growl from Tinker had been sufficient to send the darkie scuttling about his duties like a scared rabbit. Blake said nothing to Tinker about his interview with the stationmaster beyond remarking that their captive had descended from the presidential train, and adding that they would have a clear line for their run into Puerta Barrios.

They dined quickly; then, as soon as things were packed up, Tinker switched on the head and tail lamps, and they, chugged out of the siding on to the main line. They were given their clearance by a very dejected-looking stationmaster, then they were away; and, with Blake driving the car at full speed, they started, not a single word being exchanged the whole sixty miles as they went rushing through the dark walls of banana-trees that lined the way.

Blake had good reason for not talking. His mind was working at top pressure to devise some plan by which he could hoodwink Rymer now that the latter would be suspicious. Blake knew perfectly well that, when Rymer received no report from his spy, he would guess what had happened, and then he would take more active measures.

Blake's only chance to outwit him was to strike first and in such a way that Rymer would never suspect Blake's hand.

And by the time the car thundered into the station at Puerta Barrios, Blake had fixed on a tentative scheme which he thought held a possibility of success if he could bring it off. It was a big scheme and a daring one, but if he could swing McGregor into line he thought it might work.

That plan of Blake's was eventually to go down as a hectic landmark in the crimson history of Costa Buena.

Sexton Blake had almost succeeded in reaching his assistant's side, when the coal on which the struggling pair had been threshing about began to give way. Next moment Blake uttered a cry of horror as Tinker and the other reeled to the side of the speeding engine's tender, and then shot over the bridge into the river beneath. (*Chapter 9.*)

The Ninth Chapter. In which Huxton Rymer has some thing to think about.

BLAKE did not drive the car right into Puerta Barrios. He drew up about half a mile out of the town, and between them they managed to run the car on to a siding which ended in a sandpit.

Then, leaving Tinker on guard, Blake went on foot into the town and along to the Lodge. It was by then well after midnight, and the building was in darkness, which suited Blake very well. He made his way to McGregor's private apartments in one wing of the building, and after some minutes succeeded in knocking him up. While he dressed the director listened to what Blake had to say, and by the time he had finished he not only knew what had occurred at Siquirres, but had also had an outline of Blake's plan.

Over cigarettes and coffee, which McGregor's boy prepared, they discussed long and earnestly every phase of the matter until the first faint streaks of dawn began to show through the slats of the blinds.

"It's daring, Blake, and about as audacious as the coup this man Rymer brought off. But, I believe, if we go at it the right way, it might work —that is, if you can carry out your part of the programme."

"I'll do my part all right!" responded Blake grimly.

"The chief difficulty will be in bringing the Governor of Puerta Barrios into line so that he won't suspect anything. And then, of course, General Morales may not wish to re-enter political life."

"If he is a patriot, and realises that it is his duty to do so, he will not refuse," said Blake. "Anyway, it will be my job to persuade him, and I think I shall succeed."

"Very well; I am with you. I shall begin to-day to get things moving. We ought to have everything ready in about a week."

"Yes. Get the governor to send through an invitation as soon as possible. Then, through every source you can think of, start a boom going for a presidential visit. Get all the local big-wigs interested, and line some of them up for speeches. We shall need all the music we can scrape together, and plenty of flags and bunting. Then at the psychological moment we'll spring the trap. But there mustn't be a hitch at the last moment. We've got to get Rymer started, and keep him going so he can't double on us."

"You leave that to me, Blake. You produce your man in the way you say, and I'll do my share."

"Good! Then I shall lie low until to-night, and if you will have a special ready I'll go up during the night to San Jose. I mustn't be spotted now, or the whole attempt will be useless. And now, what about this greaser Tinker captured? He must be got rid of until the show is over. We don't want him reporting to Rymer."

"Can you land him on the dock?"

"Yes."

"Well, the Reventazon sails for Bocas del Toro in about two hours. If you land him on the dock I'll have him shipped down the coast on her, and I'll see that our manager in Bocas fixes it so he can't get away until I give the word."

Blake nodded, and walked back to where he had left Tinker. They got the car on to the main line again, and Blake drove at top speed right through the town and down to the dock where the Reventazon was moored.

McGregor was waiting for them and, before anyone was aware of what was happening, a couple of sailors had carried the bound figure of the Spaniard aboard. And when the Reventazon sailed, an hour later, the man was carried away from Costa Buena, to be kept out of the way until he should be harmless.

Blake and Tinker lay low all day in McGregor's private apartments. That night they slipped quietly aboard a special train, consisting only of an engine and McGregor's private carriage, which would land them in San Jose before morning. There they went directly to the private residence of the San Jose manager of the company, and Blake lost no time in getting to work, for he had plenty to do.

Down in Puerta Barrios, McGregor was also hard at work; and a few days later, when it was publicly announced that, in response to an invitation from the governor and leading citizens of Puerta Barrios, President Butterfield would make a visit to the port, no one dreamed that the whole thing had been engineered by two Britons. Nor was it generally known that the aged General Morales had left quietly for Puerta Barrios, where he was staying incog, as a private guest of the director of the Sphinx Company.

The special train bearing the presidential party was to leave San Jose early in the morning, and was due to arrive at the port a little after four in the afternoon. On its arrival there the whole populace would be assembled to give a reception to the president, and, after an address had been read, there would be a big reception and garden-party at the governor's mansion.

In the evening there was to be a state banquet and a grand ball, to which the whole population would be invited. Rather an ambitious programme, but one which the pleasure-loving natives heartily endorsed.

On leaving San Jose, the line was to be kept clear so that the special could make a straight run to Puerta Barrios without a stop on the way. The special was to be made up of an engine and two private coaches, in the first of which would be the president and his companions, and in the second the private presidential guard of an officer and about thirty men.

Just before eight o'clock the presidential party arrived at the station in San Jose, and, as the big, bearded man led the way to his private coach, it had to be admitted that he carried his dignities well. Huxton Rymer had a fine presence, and, in his immaculate white uniform, with its splashes of crimson and gold, he was a striking figure.

With him were the two other soldiers of fortune whom he had carried into power. They too were gorgeously dressed, and quite outshone the two dark-skinned Costa Buenans who completed the party.

After inspecting the personal guard of honour, Rymer entered his carriage, followed by his companions. Then the guard filed into the rear coach, and the signal was given that all was ready.

Up in the engine, the driver was leaning out of his cab, gazing back towards the station, and, as the last soldier disappeared from view, he turned and said something to the fireman, a young husky, who was covered with grease and oil.

Following this the fireman dropped to the ground on the off-side of the engine, and, running back beside the coaches, dived in between them. He bent down, and with a quick twist, disengaged the air-brake coupling, an act which no one on the station platform seemed to notice. Then he ran back and climbed into the engine.

A moment later the special conductor blew his whistle, and, to the accompaniment of the cheers of the multitude, the presidential train pulled out on its run to Puerta Barrios. And little did that fickle crowd dream that it was the last time they were to set eyes on the new president who had captured their fancy in such a short time.

The train made the long climb of twelve miles to the divide at

Cartago at a steady pace. There some of the people had gathered to give the president a cheer as he passed through, and, as he heard the voices, the grimy, bearded engine-driver smiled to himself.

He and the young fireman exchanged glances, but said nothing.

Once over the divide, it was a steady drop of five thousand feet in the next sixty-two miles to the low country, and, since the line followed the course of a river, it was almost continually twisting about precipitous gorges —one of the finest bits of scenery to be found anywhere in the world.

And it needed a steady hand to handle a train during that drop.

After leaving Cartago the train ran for nearly fifty miles at a steady clip. It was when they were passing through some rugged wild country, and where, here and there, an upgrade had to be negotiated, that the engineer turned to his young companion and uttered the single word, "Now!"

Immediately the young man began to climb over the coal in the tender, and, a few seconds later, he disappeared from view. He made his way over the rear of the tender and on to the roof of the presidential coach. He negotiated this in safety, and crossed the gap to the platform of the end coach in which were the soldiers.

Here he had to proceed very cautiously, for his object seemed to be to get down between the two coaches. He managed to do so, and, while he hung on with one hand, he worked away at the couplings with the other.

Standing thus, he waited until there came a single toot from the engine, and immediately the train slackened speed a little. In doing so the front coach fell back, as it were, against the other, and in that moment the strain on the coupling slackened.

It was just long enough for the young fireman to remove the pin, then, as the train gathered speed again, he swung to the rear platform of the first coach and began climbing to the top, while, behind him, the second coach, now detached from the train, began to slow down on the slight upgrade.

It was a nervy and clever bit of "cutting out."

Needless to say, the engineer in charge of the presidential train was Sexton Blake, and the young fireman was Tinker. The cutting out of the coach carrying the guard was but the first step in Blake's plan, and when he looked back and saw that the lad had succeeded, he pulled the throttle wide open, and they went thundering down the last few miles of the drop into the flat country at a terrific pace.

Tinker was on top of the single coach now remaining when they thundered through Siquirres and started along the run through the flat banana country. He didn't know if those inside the presidential coach were yet aware that the other coach had been left behind, but he knew it must soon be discovered, and he was anxious to get back to the engine before discovery came.

As he reached the front end of the coach he could see into the cab, and waved his hand to Blake. Blake made a sign for him to come cautiously, and Tinker jumped lightly across the gap, landing on the heaped-up coal in the tender.

He balanced himself for a second and started to cross the coal, when he heard a shout above the roar of the engine. He glanced up, and saw Blake making frantic signals to him.

He turned quickly, just in time to see Rymer and the other two Europeans crowding on to the front platform of the coach. He knew now that they had found out that the other coach had been cut off, and was by then standing isolated many miles back on the line. And he knew that, with the discovery, Huxton Rymer would not be slow to truth.

Nor was he, for now Rymer knew that the train in which he was travelling was in the control of Sexton Blake, and he began to suspect more than a little about the reception that had been planned for him in Puerto Barrios. Huxton Rymer knew if he was to avoid disaster, he would have to settle Blake before they reached the port. He didn't know just what game Blake was playing, but he could guess that it boded ill for himself.

This he conveyed in a few words to his two companions as they crowded on to the platform, and, with an oath, the adventurer, Starr, made a leap for the tender, followed by Baker.

Tinker made an effort to reach the cab, for, although Blake had drawn his revolver, he dared not shoot then for fear of hitting the lad. But Fate, in the form of a lump of coal, was Tinker's undoing. He slipped and went to his knees, and before he could recover himself, Starr was upon him.

Tinker, seeing that he would have to fight for it, turned, and as the adventurer reached for him, he drove his fist with all his strength full into Starr's solar plexus. The blow staggered the older man, but it did not stop him, and the next moment he and Tinker were struggling together in a precarious position on the top of the coal.

Baker was behind Starr, and Rymer was crouching on the back of the tender, watching the progress of the fight, and waiting to get a shot at Blake. Blake could not shoot, and he saw his only way to help Tinker was to join in the fray.

He started from the cab, and began to climb up the coal. Rymer, seeing his object, bent to one side and began taking pot shots at him. But Blake kept on, and had almost reached his objective, when the train, which had been running at reduced speed, thundered on to the long bridge which crosses the Matina River.

It was then the two struggling figures lurched backwards, and Blake saw Baker take up a huge lump of coal and hold it ready to bring down on Tinker's head as soon as he got an opportunity. The sight sent a surge of rage through Blake, and he shouted to Tinker to hold on. Disregarding the stream of bullets which Rymer was pumping towards the cab, Blake made a final effort to reach the lad. He had almost succeeded in doing so, when the coal on which the struggling pair had been threshing about began to give way, and the next moment Blake uttered a cry of horror as the pair reeled to the side and then shot over, disappearing from view like two grotesque marionettes.

Baker uttered an oath, and heaved the block of coal full at Blake. It caught Blake in the chest and drove him back, but he recovered; and now, with no fear of hitting Tinker, he jerked his revolver up and sent a bullet clean through Baker's heart. The adventurer shot over the side and disappeared, just as Tinker and Starr had, Huxton Rymer, seeing the fate of his two companions, emptied the clip of his automatic at Blake; then, with a snarl, he came over the coal to the cab. Sexton Blake was only too ready to come to grips, and as Rymer jumped down, Blake met him with a hard right to the jaw that sent the adventurer reeling. He recovered himself instantly, however, and the pair of powerful men crashed together in a struggle.

Both knew that if he would win he must win soon. They were only some twenty miles from Puerta Barrios now, and the issue must be settled before they reached the port.

It wasn't hard now for Rymer to guess what game Blake was playing, and the realisation that his old enemy had again interfered in his affairs, and was attempting to spoil the finest graft he had ever hit upon, filled him with a white-hot rage.

As for Blake, he was cool enough, but in a frenzy of anxiety over the fate of Tinker. It was sufficient for him to know that it was through Rymer that the lad had plunged over the bridge to make him determined that Rymer should pay to the uttermost for any harm the lad had suffered.

On the front platform of the coach the two Costa Buenans were standing, appalled and amazed at the scene before them. But they did not attempt to take part, which, had they but known it, was well for them.

As the engine ground on its way slowly, and without a hand at the throttle, the two combatants fought there in all that grime and heat for the mastery. It was a fight without pause, and regardless of any accepted rules. It was a sheer physical orgy for supremacy, and each man knew that the first to yield ever so slightly would be the vanquished.

Blake had followed up his attack with a fury that had kept Rymer on the defensive, and he did not abate that fury a single jot. It was his game to prevent Rymer from coming back, and in this he succeeded, though at a terrible effort. They rocked back and forth from the cab into the tender, and then into the cab. One moment it seemed as if Rymer would succeed, then Blake appeared to have the upper hand.

It was when the train swung round a wide curve that they fell apart for a moment. Then there followed a period of heavy give and take, during which both men were punished. Again the train lurched as it came once more into the straight, and as he swayed to one side Blake drove a right hook to the "button" with the whole strength of his shoulder behind it. At the moment the blow started, Rymer had been swaying towards him, with the result that the impact was terrific. No jaw of man could have withstood that blow. It sent Rymer down as if he had been hit by a thunderbolt, and after one spasmodic kick he lay still.

Sexton Blake, panting heavily, lurched into the cab and closed the throttle. Then he jammed on the brakes, and as soon as the train came to a stop he opened a locker and took out some rope, with which he securely bound the unconscious Rymer. Next, he picked up his revolver, and climbed up the heap of coal until he could cover the two Costa Buenans.

"Better go back into the coach, senores," he said curtly. "You will understand matters when we arrive in Puerta Barrios." And, having already witnessed the prowess of the grim-visaged man with the gun, they obeyed.

Blake returned to the cab, and, loosing the brakes, reversed the engine. He ran back towards Matina at a good clip, keeping his head out the whole way to see if there were any signs of Tinker or Starr, he knew he needn't worry looking for Baker.

He had almost reached the bridge when he saw a solitary figure trudging along beside the track, and as he recognised Tinker he gave an exclamation of relief. Five minutes later the lad was back in the cab, being anxiously questioned by Blake.

"Badly bruised, guv'nor, but still in the ring. That was some fall, believe me. We landed plump in the middle of the river, and had to break apart. I reached this bank, and he managed to make the other. The last I saw of him he was making into the bananas."

"Thank Heaven, my lad! I was terribly anxious about you!"

"You seem to have had a little excitement yourself," remarked Tinker, as he gazed down at Rymer, who was a strange contrast, in his torn and begrimed uniform, to the spruce individual who had boarded the train in San Jose.

"We had a little argument," admitted Blake grimly, and that was about all he ever said about the fight.

Blake took the throttle again, and drove at full speed for Puerta Barrios. As they approached the station, he saw that practically the whole population was gathered there to receive the president. But it was a very puzzled crowd that saw the special continue right on through the station, down the line to the big iron banana dock. Nor did they know that as soon as the train came to a stop there, a very battered figure was lifted out and dumped into the same motor-launch which he had once used for his own purposes.

But this time there was no bribery. The launch, with Sexton Blake and McGregor on board to see that nothing went wrong, dashed out to sea to where a Sphinx fruit-steamer had been lying anchored all day. There, in precisely the same way he had got rid of the two Gomez brothers and Montero, was Rymer bundled on board, and, without any delay the fruit boat hauled in her anchor, and steamed off on her way to the United States.

At this same moment, from the balcony of the Lodge, which overlooked the crowd that had gathered, a white-haired gentleman, whom nearly everyone recognised as the judge of the High Court in

San Jose, and, therefore, one to be accorded every respect, held up his hand for silence. Then he began to speak. He gave a brief sketch of the past history of Costa Buena.

He spoke of the long line of illustrious men who had occupied the presidential chair. Then he came to the present, and scathingly denounced the political adventurers, like Gomez and Montero, who had played battledore and shuttlecock with the highest office in the gift of the people. From that he went on to speak of the three foreign adventurers who had seized power, and were milking the country dry for their own benefit. And then, just when he knew the psychological moment had come, he said:

"You are gathered here to do homage to the president of your country. He who called himself president, the foreign adventurer who would have taken your homage to-day, is there" —and he pointed to the boat out at sea— "and will never return. But the man to whom you should do homage is here —a man who has been a father to you all, a man whose illustrious record marks him as a true patriot. Let us finish with foreign adventurers. Let us give to our own most distinguished son the greatest gift we have!

"Citizens of Costa Buena, I call upon you to salute your rightful president, the illustrious and upright man in whom we can trust. I call upon you to salute his Excellency, General Juan Morales, President of the Republic of Costa Buena! Long live the president!"

And as he paused to bring out the fine-looking old gentleman, whom the crowd recognised as their former idol, a great shout went up that left no room for doubt as to their feelings. Then the festivities, which had been ostensibly planned for one, were begun in honour of another, and by the time McGregor, Blake, and Tinker reached the Lodge, the coup had been accomplished.

And little did any in that fickle crowd realise that the grease-begrimed pair who slipped quietly into the Lodge, had engineered the whole affair.

Less than a week after the coup had been clinched in San Jose, and the new president was firmly in the saddle, the fantastic import tax on railway-sleepers, and the export tax on bananas was removed, and the Sphinx Company began again to function normally. Needless to say, Sexton Blake and Tinker were given a memorable send-off by the officials of the company when they departed for England.

Blake was well content with the success of his mission, for he knew what would have been the suffering of the great number of widows and orphans if the Sphinx Company had been forced to sustain those burdens. But all those same shareholders ever knew of the details was at the next annual meeting of the company, when Mr. Benjafield, in his address, remarked at one point:

"I am pleased to say that the various taxes which were handicapping our business in Costa Buena have been removed by the new Government, and it is entirely due to the efforts of one of our debenture holders, Mr. Sexton Blake, that this has come about. I am sure—"

As for Rymer, he dropped out of sight in New Orleans, while Starr was reported as having been seen in Nicaragua. Nothing was ever heard of Baker, who had tried to kill Tinker; but neither Blake nor Tinker wondered at that, for both knew that there are plenty of alligators in the Matina River.

They were move concerned in wondering where Huxton Rymer would pop up next.

THE END.
[20500 WORDS]

Volume *ONE* *of* *the* **DETECTIVE** **MAGAZINE** **SUPPLEMENT** will be completed with the last issue for 1923 — week ending December 29th. It will then consist of about 670 pages. The New Year will start Volume Two. Those who have been collecting the "Supplements" as they appeared will know what a magnificent book they will form when bound.

Are your Back Numbers Complete?

If not, and there are gaps you want to fill, other readers can help you. If you require any back issues of the Supplement —or complete U.J.'s —send in an application to the Editor for a Reader's Small Advert.

(See page 25.)

BACK NUMBERS.

The Editor will be pleased to publish, free of charge, any reader's announcement for the sale, purchase, or exchange of back numbers. Letters should be addressed: The Editor, UNION JACK, The Fleetway House, Farringdon Street, London, E.C. 4. It should be mentioned that advertisements other than those concerning back numbers— such as correspondents wanted and the like—cannot be published. This column is intended primarily for those who wish to fill up gaps in their collection of " U. J." Supplements, etc.

FOR SALE.

Supplement Nos. 1—73. Post free, 7s. 6d.—Leonard Packman, 130A, Copleston Road, Grove Vale, London, S.E. 15.

Supplement Nos. 1—70; also U. J. Nos. 1,009—1,038. The lot, 8s., or nearest offer.—W. Danks, 14, Chapel Lane Terrace, Saltelhebble, Halifax, Yorks.

Supplement Nos. 23—31; U. J. Nos. 1,014—1,036, with Supps.; six boxers' photos from U. J. The lot, 3s. 6d. Also complete set Champion photos in album; post free, 5s. 6d.—Gladys Daniels, 82, Abingdon Road, Oxford.

U. J. 200 Nos, misc. Write for list.—J. Winslade, 19, Lower Thames Street, Merthyr Tydvil, South Wales.

U. J. and B. F. Lib. and others, from 1907 to date. Send stamp for list.—J. Lloyd, 30, Machen Place, Riverside, Cardiff.

U. J. and S. B. Lib., Boys' Friend, Nelson Lee Lib., Gem, Magnet, Popular. Odd numbers, half price. Send stamp for list.—R. V. Mayner, St. Helens, Purewell, Christchurch, Hants.

U. J., Sexton Blake Lib., and others. Write for list.—E. Bracken, Belan Moone, Ballytore, Kildare, Ireland.

S. B. Lib., fourteen odd numbers; the lot, 3s.—W. Wilson, Wancop, Penryth, Westmorland.

S. B. Lib., Nos. 293, 296, 297, 300, 301. Write offer.—K. N. Dark, 66, St. Mary's Street, Chippenham, Wilts.

U. J., complete with Supp., but without football coupons. Misc. numbers. Write for list.—T. Roberts, 33, Maude Street, New Basford.

U. J. Nos. 1,012—1,032, with Treasure Island serial complete, 2s.— K. Davis, Hayden Avenue, Moss-side, Manchester.

Supplement Nos. 1—72; No. 9 missing. Coloured plate Sexton Blake, complete series boxers' photos, Police of all Nations (No. 6 missing), 3s. 6d., postage included—G. Read, 47, Peel Lane, Partick, Glasgow.

U. J. and S. B. Lib. from 1918; misc. numbers. Write for list.— N. Vandamme, Duncliffe, 11, Rosebery Road, Boscombe, Hants.

U. J. Nos. 946 onwards (No. 1,000 missing), without supplements. Also odd numbers Boys' Cinema, Girls' Cinema, Girls' Favourite, Magnet, Gem, Champion, Popular.—J. Maniourian, Souk-el-thabb- hine, Heddeni Buildings, Alexandria, Egypt.

S. B. Lib., 100 odd numbers. B. F. Lib., 100 odd numbers. All at 3d. each.—R. E. Rowe, Bridge Cottage, 1, St. John's Road, Helston, Yorks.

WANTED.

U. J. No. 1,000. 6d. offered.—W. Wilson, Wancop, Penryth, Westmorland.

Supplements Nos. 1—73. Set of boxers and Police of all Nations. —C. Sharp, 52, Ash Road, Stratford, London, E. 15.

S. B. Lib., misc. numbers. Willing to pay 1s. each. Early numbers only, not beyond 34. Write specifying numbers available. —H. Creswell, 15, Cliff Road, Cromer.

EXCHANGE.

U. J. from 995—1,040, without Supps. Will exchange for Supps. Nos. 1—18.—F. Gartlan, 70, Smithdown Lane, Edgehill, Liverpool.

www.ingramcontent.com/pod-product-compliance
Lightning Source LLC
Chambersburg PA
CBHW020342130626
46549CB00003B/1252